Luna's Star

Sheamus Rasch

ISBN 978-1-888215-41-0 (paperback)

ISBN 978-1-888215-42-7 (ebook)

Library of Congress Control Number: 2020924715

Publisher's Cataloging-in-Publication data

Names: Rasch, Sheamus, author.

Title: Luna's star / Sheamus Rasch.

Description: Anchorage, AK: Fathom Publishing Company, 2020. | Summary: The adventures of an owlet who dreamed of reaching the stars.

Identifiers: LCCN: 2020924715 | ISBN 978-1-888215-41-0 (pbk.) | 978-1-888215-42-7 (ebook)

Subjects: LCSH Owls--Juvenile fiction. | Space flight--Juvenile fiction. | Astronauts--Juvenile fiction. | Family--Juvenile fiction. | CYAC Owls--Fiction. | Space flight-- Fiction. | Astronauts-- Fiction. | Family-- Fiction. | BISAC JUVENILE FICTION / Animals / Birds | JUVENILE FICTION / Science Fiction / Space Exploration | JUVENILE FICTION / Animals / Baby Animals

Classification: LCC PZ7.1 .R37 Lun 2020 | DDC (E)--dc23

Printed in the United States

Fathom Publishing Company

PO Box 200448 | Anchorage, Alaska 99520

www.FathomPublishing.com

www.SeamusRaschBooks.com

Dedication

Dedicated to my found family
who never stopped believing in me.

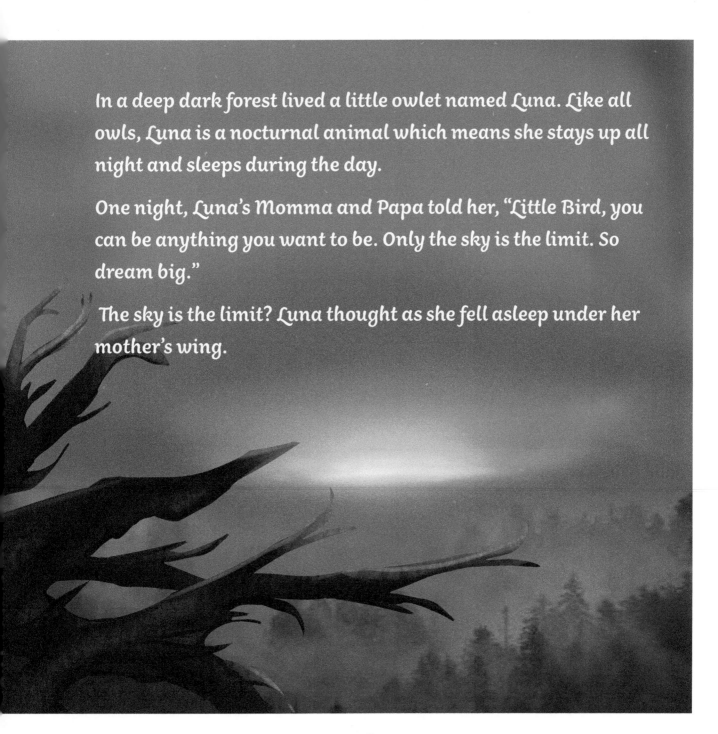

In a deep dark forest lived a little owlet named Luna. Like all owls, Luna is a nocturnal animal which means she stays up all night and sleeps during the day.

One night, Luna's Momma and Papa told her, "Little Bird, you can be anything you want to be. Only the sky is the limit. So dream big."

The sky is the limit? Luna thought as she fell asleep under her mother's wing.

And dream big she did. Luna dreamed a dream while she slept through the day. She dreamed that she flew up very high and far away. So high in fact that she could touch the stars.

Then Luna said, "I know! I will fly very high and get a star and give it to my family! That would be the most amazing gift for the most amazing Momma and Papa. They would be so proud of me."

But how do you fly up that high? Luna thought. Each night she watched Momma and Papa fly very high, but they never flew close enough to touch the stars. It seemed impossible. She needed to think bigger. Grandpa Owl was very wise. He knew all kinds of things. She climbed down from the nest and went over to ask him how to reach the stars.

"Silly Owlet. Stars live past the clouds in the sky. We live on earth and they live in space. Only astronauts can go to space."

"Okay, then, I will become an astronaut!" said the little owl.

So, she left her nest and went to school where anyone could learn to be anything.

She studied very hard. She read, and she read, and she read.

9

She read and read and read until her head spun. She
learned all kinds of things. She learned how to paint. She
learned how to add and subtract. She learned all about the
world.

The teachers and other kids were very amazed.

"Wow, you are so smart, Luna! Do you want to play with us?" the other kids asked.

"Play? Oh, that sounds nice. Maybe later. If I want to be an astronaut, I need to study a lot!"

Luna studied until her head spun. She studied until her wings grew big and beautiful. But she did not stop until the teacher said, "Luna, you have read every book in this classroom. If you want to go to space, you have learned everything you would need to know."

All the other animals in the forest and all the students and teachers in the school gathered around to watch as the tiny owl built an owl-sized rocket ship. She even made her very own space suit just so she could go to space and collect her star.

The day finally came. Three ... Two ... One ... Blast off! Luna hit the big green button. The rocket ship launched into space! This was it! All her studying was over.

Now she could finally get her very own star. Luna's ship was flying past all the other birds in the night sky. It flew past the clouds. She flew up so high until her home and everyone she knew looked like a tiny toy set.

She kept soaring fast towards the stars until the earth was far away. She finally made it into space!

It was like a big black ocean full of glitter. It was beautiful, but she still could not find a star to grab. They seemed very far away.

Luna began to become very frustrated. She kept flying farther and farther into space. It was very quiet. The Earth looked like a tiny dot. There were no owls hooting, no crickets chirping, no bumbling rivers and no stories from Grandpa Owl. Luna closed her eyes and tried to remember all of the hugs from her Momma and Papa.

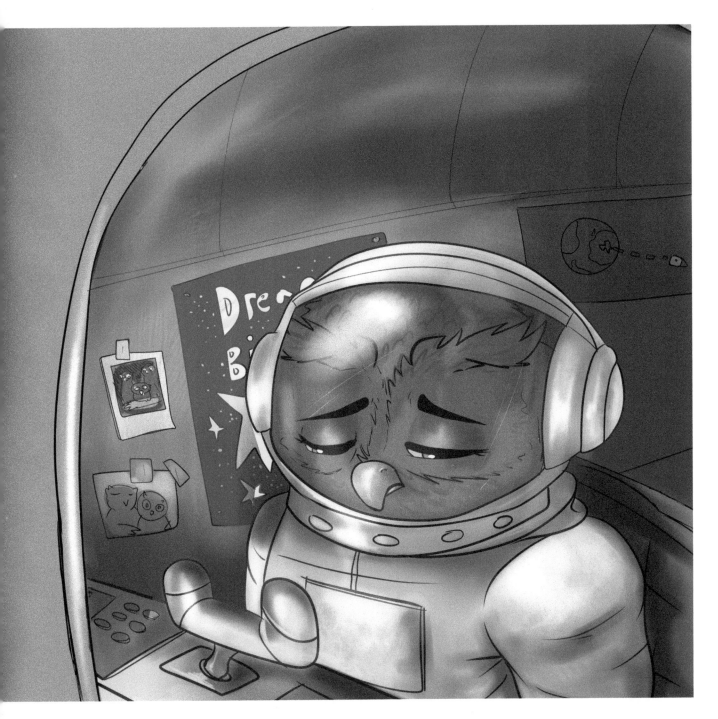

Bang! While Luna was sitting with her eyes closed, a giant space rock called an asteroid crashed into her ship! Luna's ship was pushed backward towards Earth.

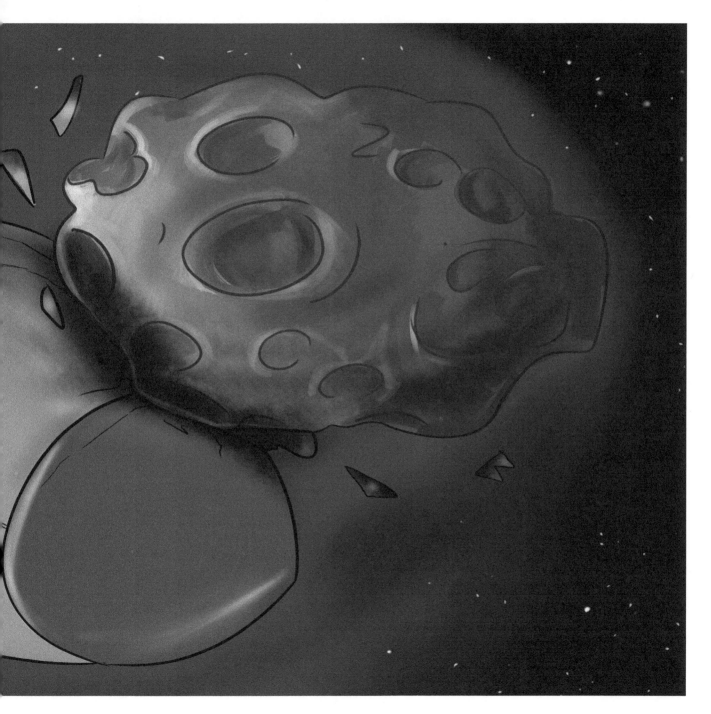

Luna hit the big red button on her spaceship, opening the emergency exit. She jumped out of the ship and flapped her wings as hard as she could. Back on earth, Momma and Papa watched the spaceship crash.

"Oh no! What happened to our Luna?" they both yelled.

"I am right here, Momma and Papa!"

Luna was now a grown-up owl. She had big wings. She flew to her parents.

"Thank the stars you are okay!" Momma said.

"I'm sorry!" Luna cried. "Space was amazing, but I did not get you a star like I promised."

"Well, you flew all the way to space, didn't you?" asked Momma.

"Yes" said Luna.

"And isn't that where stars come from?" Papa asked.

"Yes." Said Luna.

"Then you must be our star. The star we have been waiting for to you bring back! Then Momma gave Luna a special gold star necklace. Papa gave Luna a big hug.

Glossary

Amaze: to fill with wonder

Asteroid: rocky objects floating in space that orbit the sun, usually found between the orbits of Mars and Jupiter

Astronaut: a person who trains to travel into space

Frustrate: to cause feelings of discouragement

Nocturnal: happening at night

Owlet: a small or young owl

Space: the area outside the earth's atmosphere where there is no air

Star: a glowing ball of hot gas in space; our sun is a star

About the Author

Sheamus Rasch is a born and raised Alaskan resident with a lifelong passion for music, cartoons, avians, and helping others. He has been doodling comics with his friends since grade school, the bright colors and stories contrasting the dark and cold winters of the north. By day, he works as a Licensed Massage Therapist. He lives in a lake cabin with his fiancé of eight years. This is his first published book.

SheamusRaschBooks.com

CPSIA information can be obtained
at www.ICGtesting.com
Printed in the USA
BVHW021949090121
597419BV00003B/87